It's Heaven to Be Seven

It's Heaven to Be Seven

A
LITTLE APPLE
PAPERBACK

SCHOLASTIC INC.
New York Toronto London Auckland Sydney
Mexico City New Delhi Hong Kong

24 23 22 21 20 19 18 17 16   6 7 8 9/0

Printed in the U.S.A.   40

First Scholastic printing, October 1999

Contents

Introduction   vii

1. From *The One in the Middle Is the Green Kangaroo* by Judy Blume   1

2. From *James and the Giant Peach* by Roald Dahl   8

3. From *Ramona and Her Father* by Beverly Cleary   14

4. From *Pinky and Rex and the Bully* by James Howe   24

5. From Baby-sitters Little Sister #7: *Karen's Birthday* by Ann M. Martin   36

6. From *Seven Kisses in a Row* by Patricia MacLachlan   41

7. From *Jasper and the Hero Business* by Betty Horvath   48

8. From *New Neighbors for Nora* by Johanna Hurwitz   59

9. From *Song Lee in Room 2B* by Suzy Kline   71

10. From *Don't Call Me Beanhead!*
    by Susan Wojciechowski   83

11. From *Sophie Is Seven*
    by Dick King-Smith   94

12. From *Second-Grade Friends*
    by Miriam Cohen   102

Introduction

Congratulations! You are seven — and you are not alone. In this book you will meet lots of other seven-year-olds: shy kids, silly kids, brave kids, and scared kids . . . kids just like you. Kids in stories by your favorite authors, all written to prove that it is Heaven to Be Seven.

Of course, being seven also means being very grown-up. It means having brand-new, important feelings and wanting brand-new, important things. Like Nora, who wants a neighbor her own age to play with, and Sophie, who wants to ride a horse. Karen wants her family to be all together. Ramona wants her family to be happy again. Jasper wants to be a hero. And Pinky just wants a new name!

Being seven also means having brand-new, important adventures. Like Freddy Dissel, who has a special part in the school play; Beatrice (Beany) Sherwin-Hendricks, who really loses a tooth; and James Henry Trotter, who sets off on a peach of a journey!

Maybe you have wanted the same things. Maybe you have had the same adventures. Or maybe there are stories here that you have never dreamed of. What happens to all these seven-year-olds? There's only one way to find out. Read their stories and see!

It's Heaven
to Be Seven

From
The One in the Middle Is the Green Kangaroo
by Judy Blume

7

Lately second grader Freddy Dissel has that left-out kind of feeling. Life can be lonely when you're the middle kid in the family and you feel like "the peanut butter part of a sandwich," squeezed between an older brother and a little sister. But Freddy has a part in the school play, and for the first time it's his chance to show everyone how special he is and, most of all, prove it to himself!

The next two weeks were busy ones for Freddy. He had to practice being the Green Kangaroo a lot. He practiced at school on the stage. He practiced at home, too. He made kangaroo faces in front of the mirror. He did kangaroo jumps on his bed. He even dreamed about Green Kangaroos at night.

Finally, the day of the play came. The whole family would be there. Some of their neighbors were coming, too.

1

Mom hugged Freddy extra hard as he left for school. "We'll be there watching you, Green Kangaroo," she said.

After lunch Ms. Gumber called to Freddy. "Time to go now. Time to get into your costume." Ms. Gumber walked to the hall with Freddy.

Then she whispered, "We'll be in the second row. Break a leg."

"Break a leg?" Freddy said.

Ms. Gumber laughed. "That means good luck when you're in a play."

"Oh," Freddy said. "I thought you meant I

should fall off the stage and *really* break a leg."

Ms. Gumber laughed again. She ruffled Freddy's hair.

Freddy went to Ms. Matson's room. The girls in the sixth grade had made his costume. They all giggled when Ms. Matson helped Freddy into it. His Green Kangaroo suit covered all of him. It even had green feet. Only his face stuck out. Ms. Matson put some

green dots on it. "We'll wash them off later. Okay?"

"Okay," Freddy mumbled. He jumped over to the mirror. He looked at himself. He really felt like a Green Kangaroo.

It was time for the play to begin. Freddy waited backstage with the fifth and sixth graders who were in the play. They looked at him and smiled. He tried to smile back. But the smile wouldn't come. His heart started to beat faster. His stomach bounced up and down. He felt funny. Then Ms. Matson leaned close to him. She said, "They're waiting for you, Freddy. Go ahead."

He jumped out onto the stage. He looked out into the audience. All those people were down there — somewhere. He knew they were. It was very quiet. He could hear his heart. He thought he saw Mom and Dad. He thought he saw Ellen. He thought he saw Mike and Ms. Gumber and his second-grade class and all of his neighbors, too. They were all out there somewhere. They were all in the middle of the audience. But Freddy wasn't in the middle. He was all by himself up on the stage. He had a job to do. He *had* to be the Green Kangaroo.

Freddy smiled. His heart slowed down. His stomach stayed still. He felt better. He smiled a bigger, wider smile. He felt good.

"HELLO EVERYONE," Freddy said. "I AM THE GREEN KANGAROO. WELCOME."

The play began. Freddy did his big and little jumps. Every few minutes one of the fifth or sixth graders in the play said to him, "And who are you?"

Freddy jumped around and answered. "Me? I am the Green Kangaroo!" It was easy. That was all he had to say. It was fun, too. Every time he said it the audience laughed.

Freddy liked it when they laughed. It was a funny play.

When it was all over everyone on the stage took a bow. Then Ms. Matson came out and waited for the audience to get quiet. She said, "A special thank-you to our second grader, Freddy Dissel. He played the part of the Green Kangaroo."

Freddy jumped over to the middle of the stage. He took a big, low bow all by himself. The audience clapped hard for a long time.

From
James and the Giant Peach
by Roald Dahl

7

When he was just seven years old, some very peculiar things happened to James Henry Trotter. First, he was given some magic crystals by a very peculiar old man. Then he accidentally spilled them by the old peach tree. Then one peach grew and grew and grew until it was bigger than a house. Now James is inside the peach with his very peculiar new friends — Spider, Ladybug, Grasshopper, Centipede, and Worm — about to set off on an even more peculiar adventure.

"We're off!" someone was shouting. "We're off at last!"

James woke up with a jump and looked about him. The creatures were all out of their hammocks and moving excitedly around the room. Suddenly the floor gave a great heave, as though an earthquake were taking place.

"Here we go!" shouted the Old-Green-

Grasshopper, hopping up and down with excitement. "Hold on tight!"

"What's happening?" cried James, leaping out of his hammock. "What's going on?"

The Ladybug, who was obviously a kind and gentle creature, came over and stood beside him. "In case you don't know it," she we are about to depart forever from the top of this ghastly hill that we've all been living on for so long. We are about to roll away inside this great big beautiful peach to a land of . . . of . . . of . . . to a land of —"

"Of what?" asked James.

"Never you mind," said the Ladybug. "But nothing could be worse than this desolate hilltop and those two repulsive aunts of yours —"

"Hear, hear!" they all shouted. "Hear, hear!"

"You may not have noticed it," the Ladybug went on, "but the whole garden, even before it reaches the steep edge of the hill, happens to be on a steep slope. And therefore the only thing that has been stopping this peach from rolling away right from the beginning is the thick stem attaching it to the tree. Break the stem, and off we go!"

"Watch it!" cried Miss Spider, as the room gave another violent lurch. "Here we go!"

"Not quite! Not quite!"

"At this moment," continued the Ladybug, "our Centipede, who has a pair of jaws as sharp as razors, is up there on top of the peach nibbling away at that stem. In fact, he must be nearly through it, as you can tell from the way we're lurching about. Would you like me to take you under my wing so that you won't fall over when we start rolling?"

"That's very kind of you," said James, "but I think I'll be all right."

Just then, the Centipede stuck his grinning face through a hole in the ceiling and shouted, "I've done it! We're off!"

"We're off!" the others cried. "We're off!"

"The journey begins!" shouted the Centipede.

"And who knows where it will end," muttered the Earthworm, "if *you* have anything to do with it. It can only mean trouble."

"Nonsense," said the Ladybug. "We are now about to visit the most marvelous places and see the most wonderful things! Isn't that so, Centipede?"

"There is no knowing what we shall see!" cried the Centipede.

"We may see a Creature with forty-nine heads
Who lives in the desolate snow,
And whenever he catches a cold (which he
    dreads)
He has forty-nine noses to blow.

"We may see the venomous Pink-Spotted
    Scrunch

Who can chew up a man with one bite.
It likes to eat five of them roasted for lunch
And eighteen for its supper at night.

"We may see a Dragon, and nobody knows
That we won't see a Unicorn there.
We may see a terrible Monster with toes
Growing out of the tufts of his hair.

"We may see the sweet little Biddy-Bright Hen
So playful, so kind and well-bred;
And such beautiful eggs! You just boil them
    and then
They explode and they blow off your head.

"A Gnu and a Gnocerous surely you'll see
And that gnormous and gnorrible Gnat
Whose sting when it stings you goes in at the
    knee
And comes out through the top of your hat.

"We may even get lost and be frozen by frost.
We may die in an earthquake or tremor.
Or nastier still, we may even be tossed
On the horns of a furious Dilemma.

"But who cares! Let us go from this horrible
    hill!
Let us roll! Let us bowl! Let us plunge!

12

*Let's go rolling and bowling and spinning
    until
We're away from old Spiker and Sponge!"*

One second later . . . slowly, insidiously, oh most gently, the great peach started to lean forward and steal into motion. The whole room began to tilt over and all the furniture went sliding across the floor, and crashed against the far wall. So did James and the Ladybug and the Old-Green-Grasshopper and Miss Spider and the Earthworm, also the Centipede, who had just come slithering quickly down the wall.

From
Ramona and Her Father
by Beverly Cleary

7

Seven started off as a good year for Ramona Quimby. But then her father lost his job and everything seemed to change. Now everyone is grouchy. Even worse, her sister Beezus tells Ramona that their father's smoking will turn his lungs black and he'll die. Maybe Ramona can't help her father find a job. But she can help him stop smoking, she decides, even if she is just a second grader.

Mr. Quimby continued to smoke, and Ramona continued to worry. Then one afternoon, when Ramona came home from school, she found the back door locked. When she pounded on it with her fist, no one answered. She went to the front door, rang the doorbell, and waited. Silence. Lonely silence. She tried the door even though she knew it was locked. More silence. Nothing like this had ever happened to Ramona before. Someone was always waiting when she came home from school.

Ramona was frightened. Tears filled her eyes as she sat down on the cold concrete steps to think. Where could her father be? She thought of her friends at school, Davy and Sharon, who did not have fathers. Where had their fathers gone? Everybody had a father sometime. Where could they go?

Ramona's insides tightened with fear. Maybe her father was angry with her. Maybe he had gone away because she tried to make him stop smoking. She thought she was saving his life, but maybe she was being mean to him. Her mother said she must not annoy her father, because he was worried about being out of work. Maybe she had made him so angry he did not love her anymore. Maybe he had gone away because he did not love her. She thought of all the scary things she had seen on television — houses that had fallen down in earthquakes, people shooting people, big hairy men on motorcycles — and knew she needed her father to keep her safe.

The cold from the concrete seeped through Ramona's clothes. She wrapped her arms around her knees to keep warm as she

watched a dried leaf scratch along the driveway in the autumn wind. She listened to the honking of the flock of wild geese flying through the gray clouds on their way south for the winter. They came from Canada, her father had once told her, but that was before he had gone away. Raindrops began to dot the driveway, and tears dotted Ramona's skirt. She put her head down on her knees and cried. Why had she been so mean to her father? If he ever came back he could smoke all he wanted, fill the ashtrays and turn the air blue, and she wouldn't say a single word. She just wanted her father back, black lungs and all.

And suddenly there he was, scrunching through the leaves on the driveway with the collar of his windbreaker turned up against the wind and his old fishing hat pulled down over his eyes. "Sorry I'm late," he said, as he got out his key. "Is that what all this boohooing is about?"

Ramona wiped her sweater sleeve across her nose and stood up. She was so glad to see her father and so relieved that he had not gone away, that anger blazed up. Her tears became angry tears. Fathers were not supposed to worry their little girls. "Where have you been?" she demanded. "You're supposed to be here when I come home from school! I thought you had gone away and left me."

"Take it easy. I wouldn't go off and leave you. Why would I do a thing like that?" Mr. Quimby unlocked the door and, with a hand on Ramona's shoulder, guided her into the living room. "I'm sorry I had to worry you. I was collecting my unemployment insurance, and I had to wait in a long line."

Ramona's anger faded. She knew all about long lines and understood how difficult they were. She had waited in lines for her turn at the slides in the park, she had waited in lines in the school lunchroom back in the days when her family could spare lunch money once in a while, she had waited in lines with her mother at the check-out counter in the market, when she was little she had waited in long, long lines to see Santa Claus in the department store, and — these were the worst, most boring lines of all — she had waited in lines with her mother in the bank. She felt bad because her father had had to wait in line, and she also understood that collecting unemployment insurance did not make him happy.

"Did somebody try to push ahead of you?" Ramona was wise in the ways of lines.

"No. The line was unusually long today."

Mr. Quimby went into the kitchen to make himself a cup of instant coffee. While he waited for the water to heat, he poured Ramona a glass of milk and gave her a graham cracker.

"Feeling better?" he asked.

Ramona looked at her father over the rim of her glass and nodded, spilling milk down her front. Silently he handed her a dish towel to wipe up while he poured hot water over the instant coffee in his mug. Then he reached into his shirt pocket, pulled out a package of cigarettes, looked at it a moment, and tossed it onto the counter. Ramona had never seen her father do this before. Could it be . . .

Mr. Quimby leaned against the counter and took a sip of coffee. "What would you like to do?" he asked Ramona.

Ramona considered before she answered. "Something big and important." But what? she wondered. Break a record in that book of records Beezus talked about? Climb Mount Hood?

"Such as?" her father asked.

Ramona finished scrubbing the front of her sweater with the dish towel. "Well —" she said, thinking. "You know that big bridge across the Columbia River?"

19

"Yes. The Interstate Bridge. The one we cross when we drive to Vancouver."

"I've always wanted to stop on that bridge and get out of the car and stand with one foot in Oregon and one foot in Washington."

"A good idea, but not practical," said Mr. Quimby. "Your mother has the car, and I doubt if cars are allowed to stop on the bridge. What else?"

"It's not exactly important, but I always like to crayon," said Ramona. How long would her father leave his cigarettes on the counter?

Mr. Quimby set his cup down. "I have a

20

great idea! Let's draw the longest picture in the world." He opened a drawer and pulled out a roll of shelf paper. When he tried to unroll it on the kitchen floor, the paper rolled itself up again. Ramona quickly solved that problem by Scotch-taping the end of the roll to the floor. Together she and her father unrolled the paper across the kitchen and knelt with a box of crayons between them.

"What shall we draw?" she asked.

"How about the state of Oregon?" he suggested. "That's big enough."

Ramona's imagination was excited. "I'll begin with the Interstate Bridge," she said.

"And I'll tackle Mount Hood," said her father.

Together they went to work, Ramona on the end of the shelf paper and her father halfway across the kitchen. With crayons Ramona drew a long black bridge with a girl standing astride a line in the center. She drew blue water under the bridge, even though the Columbia River always looked gray. She added gray clouds, gray dots for raindrops, and all the while she was drawing she was trying to find courage to tell her father something.

Ramona glanced at her father's picture, and sure enough he had drawn Mount Hood peaked with a hump on the south side exactly the way it looked in real life on the days when the clouds lifted.

"I think you draw better than anybody in the whole world," said Ramona.

Mr. Quimby smiled. "Not quite," he said.

"Daddy —" Ramona summoned courage. "I'm sorry I was mean to you."

"You weren't mean." Mr. Quimby was adding trees at the base of the mountain. "You're right, you know."

"Am I?" Ramona wanted to be sure.

"Yes."

This answer gave Ramona even more

courage. "Is that why you didn't have a cigarette with your coffee? Are you going to stop smoking?"

"I'll try," answered Mr. Quimby, his eyes on his drawing. "I'll try."

Ramona was filled with joy, enthusiasm, and relief. "You can do it, Daddy! I know you can do it."

Her father seemed less positive. "I hope so," he answered, "but if I succeed, Picky-picky will still have to eat Puss-puddy."

"He can try, too," Ramona said, and slashed dark V's across her gray sky to represent a flock of geese flying south for the winter.

From
Pinky and Rex and the Bully
by James Howe

7

Pinky has big problems. Pink is his favorite color, and Kevin, the third-grade bully, says this makes him a sissy. Pinky's best friend, Rex, is a girl, and Kevin says this will make Pinky turn into a girl, too. What is a seven-year-old boy to do?

That night after dinner, Pinky was helping his father clean up. "Is it bad that I like pink?" he asked.

"Of course not," his father said. "Pink has always been your favorite color."

"Yeah, but now that I'm seven maybe I should like a different color."

"What does being seven have to do with it?"

Pinky put down his dish towel and slumped into a chair. Finally, he said, "Maybe you shouldn't call me Pinky anymore."

"When you were little, we called you Billy," his father said.

24

Pinky thought for a long time. Then he said, "From now on, I'm Billy."

Later, in his room, Pinky looked at all his stuffed animals. Every one of them had pink on it somewhere. He could just imagine what Kevin would say about them. He picked up his favorite, Pretzel the pig.

"Hi, Pretzel," he said. "I'm Billy now." The name felt funny in his mouth. "I guess I have to make some other changes, too. I just want

you to know that no matter what happens, you'll always be my friend."

"I heard you and Daddy talking before."

Pinky turned as his little sister Amanda came into his room and flopped down on the bed. "Well, I'm not going to call you Billy."

"You have to because that's my name from now on," he told her.

Amanda shrugged. "Okay, but then you have to give me your animals."

"Why?"

"Because if you're not going to be called

Pinky anymore, then you can't like pink anymore. And if you don't like pink anymore,
then you can't have these animals anymore."

Pinky thought about what his sister said.
Then he gave her every one of his stuffed animals.

That night, he woke up several times. He

looked around his empty room and wondered where he was.

The next day was Saturday. Pinky didn't want to get up. He had something very hard to do that morning — maybe the hardest thing he would ever have to do in his whole life. After he heard Amanda go downstairs, he sneaked into her bedroom.

"Hi, Pretzel," he whispered. "Did you miss me?"

He made Pretzel's head nod yes.

"I'm supposed to play with Rex today," he told his friend with the curly tail, "but I have to tell her I can't play with her anymore. Why? Because she's a girl, Pretzel, don't you understand?"

He made Pretzel's head move from side to side.

"That's because you're a pig. If you were a boy like me, you'd know that you're not supposed to be friends with girls. I mean, it's okay when you're a little kid, but not when you're seven."

Pretzel looked at Pinky with blank button eyes.

It was almost noon by the time Pinky was dressed and out of the house. Standing at the end of Rex's sidewalk, he tried to figure out the words he would say to her. None of them seemed right.

"Why, hello there, Pinky," he heard Mrs. Morgan call out. She was sitting on her front porch, looking through her mail.

"My name is Billy now," he told her.

"What's that?"

Pinky went to Mrs. Morgan's porch and sat on the top step. "I said my name is Billy," he repeated.

"Oh, you don't want to be called Pinky anymore?"

Pinky shook his head.

"I see," Mrs. Morgan said. "And why is that?"

"Because I don't like pink," Pinky told her. "And a boy shouldn't have a pink bike. And Pinky is a dumb name for a boy. And a boy shouldn't play with girls."

"My goodness," Mrs. Morgan said. "I had no idea there were so many rules for boys. Imagine if you still *did* like pink and you *wanted* to be Rex's friend. How hard it would be to have to pretend to follow all those rules."

"I don't make the rules," Pinky said.

"Oh," said Mrs. Morgan. "Then who does?"

Pinky didn't have an answer for that.

"You know, Pinky, I mean Billy, when I

was young I decided to follow the rules, too. Other people's rules, I mean. It was a very silly thing to do."

"Why?" Pinky asked.

"Do you remember my telling you that I used to paint pictures? Well, I loved to paint so much it was all I wanted to do. But some of the other children made fun of me. They stuck their noses in the air and called me 'the artist.' That hurt. Because as much as I loved to paint, I hated feeling different.

"So one day, I put away all my brushes and I never took them out again. I pretended I liked doing the things the other children liked to do.

"Soon they stopped making fun of me. And over time I forgot all about painting. Then the other day I was looking at that beautiful pink bush and it all came back to me. And, oh, the sadness that came with it."

Mrs. Morgan paused. "I know why that bully pushed you down," she went on. "It's

hard to be different, isn't it, Billy? And have other children make fun of you. But, believe me, it's worse not to be yourself. Don't change for other people, Billy. Other people will come and go in your life. Do what's right for the one person who will always be with you — yourself."

Pinky sat for a long time, thinking. When he saw Rex come out of her house, he stood up.

"Going to play now, Billy?" Mrs. Morgan asked.

He nodded, then turned back. "I don't think I want to be called Billy," he said. "Okay?"

Mrs. Morgan smiled. "Okay, Pinky. Now, run along. Your friend is waiting."

From
Baby-sitters Little Sister #7:
Karen's Birthday
by Ann M. Martin

7

Karen Brewer, star of the Baby-sitters Little Sister series, is very excited. She is turning seven. That must make you very grown-up, she thinks. After all, last year, when she turned six, all she wanted was parties and presents. But this year Karen wants something very different.

Of course, there was no way Daddy could have guessed what I wanted to do for my birthday. That was because I had not given anybody any hints. And I could tell that Daddy really wanted to take my friends and me to the circus. Daddy *loves* circuses. And he knew that I wanted to go to the Happy-Time Circus . . . but not for my birthday.

"Oh, Daddy," I said. I tried to sound excited. "Thank you. The circus would be . . . neat. But I haven't thought much about my birthday." That was a big lie. I had been thinking about my birthday forever. "Can I decide about the circus in a little while?" I asked him.

Daddy said I could take my time deciding. Then we hung up the phone. I went to my bedroom. I took Emily Junior out of her cage and put her on my lap. Emily Junior is my rat. (She is named after my adopted sister.)

I sat and thought. I thought about my birthday and the circus and being a two-two.

What is a two-two? A two-two is someone like Andrew and me who has two of everything because their parents are divorced. I got the name from a book my teacher read to our class. It was called *Jacob Two-Two Meets the Hooded Fang*. I thought "two-two" described my brother and me perfectly. I am Karen Two-Two. Andrew is Andrew Two-Two.

See, a long time ago my mommy and daddy used to be married. Then they got divorced. Then they each got married again. Mommy married Seth. He is my stepfather. Daddy married Elizabeth. She is my stepmother. Andrew and I live with Mommy and Seth most of the time. But every other weekend, and for two weeks during the summer, we live with Daddy and Elizabeth.

Mommy and Seth live in a little house. No one else lives there except Andrew and me, and Rocky and Midgie and Emily Junior.

(Rocky and Midgie are Seth's cat and dog.) The little house is usually quiet.

Daddy and Elizabeth live in a huge house. It is a mansion. And it is noisy because lots of people are always around. For one thing, Elizabeth has four kids of her own. They are Sam and Charlie, who are so big they're in high school, and Kristy, who is thirteen and one of my most favorite people. (She is a good baby-sitter as well as a nice stepsister.) There is also David Michael. He's seven. As soon as I have my birthday, we'll be the same age. Then there is Emily Michelle. She's the one I named my rat after. Daddy and Elizabeth adopted her. She is two years old and came from a faraway country called Vietnam. Last but not least, there is Nannie. She is Elizabeth's mother, which makes her my step-grandmother. She helps take care of all of us. Oh, I almost forgot. There are also two pets — Shannon, David Michael's puppy, and Boo-Boo, Daddy's fat, mean cat.

Andrew and I have everything we need at each house. We have toys at each house. We have bicycles at each house. We have clothes and friends and mommies and daddies and stuffed animals at each house. Two of everything. That is why we are two-twos.

Being a two-two might sound like fun, and

it can be. But here is one thing I do not like about being a two-two: I never get to see everybody in my *whole* family at once. I either see the little-house family or the big-house family. So what I had decided I wanted for my birthday was to invite all the people at the little house and all the people at the big house to one party. I just wanted us to be together.

That was why I didn't sound so happy when Daddy asked if I wanted to take some of my friends to the Happy-Time Circus. It meant that once again Daddy was planning one party and Mommy was planning another.

And that was not what I wanted.

From
Seven Kisses in a Row
by Patricia MacLachlan

7

It just isn't fair! How could Emma's parents leave her and her brother Zachary for five whole days with her Aunt Evelyn and Uncle Elliot? She hardly knows them. And they don't know anything about being parents — things like divided grapefruit with a cherry in the middle for breakfast or seven kisses in a row in the morning. And that is just the beginning.

Aunt Evelyn and Uncle Elliot came with lots of rules. Rules about eating: how much and what to. Rules about sleeping: what time and how to. They had rules about cleaning and messing up, playing and resting, how to dress and when to.

In the morning Aunt Evelyn and Uncle Elliot exercised. Emma and Zach's parents did not exercise. They ran about a lot, but they did not call it exercising.

"Exercising twice a day is one of my rules," explained Uncle Elliot. "Once in the morning, once at night." He wore a torn sweat shirt and matching torn pants as he ran in place in front of the television. He made the same kinds of *oosh*ing sounds that he made when he slept. Aunt Evelyn did not make *oosh*ing sounds. She made no sounds at all as she bent her legs and arms in odd ways. First Aunt Evelyn twisted herself into the shape of a swan. Then a large U. Then a pretzel.

"Do you like what you're doing?" asked Emma.

"I love it!" exclaimed Aunt Evelyn. "It makes me feel like a bird. Free. Soaring! You should try it."

Emma did try it. But it didn't make her feel much like a bird. It hurt.

"Does Uncle Elliot like to exercise, too?" asked Zachary.

"NO!" shouted Uncle Elliot, *oosh*ing in front of the morning news. "But it's one of my rules, exercising is."

"I'll run with you," said Zachary. "We could run around the block."

"The block! That's a good idea," said Uncle Elliot. "We'll take the dog, too. Dogs love to run."

"Not Wayne," said Emma. "Wayne only likes to sit. Or lie down."

"Nonsense," said Uncle Elliot. He snapped the leash on Wayne's collar. Wayne lay down. "Come, Wayne! Up, Wayne! Run, Wayne!" urged Uncle Elliot. He pulled while Zachary pushed Wayne from behind. When they left, Emma and Aunt Evelyn smiled at each other.

"What would you like to do now?" asked Aunt Evelyn. "Maybe you have homework to do."

"It's only Saturday morning," said Emma. "I always do my homework late Sunday night."

Aunt Evelyn frowned. "Late Sunday night? When I was your age we had a rule to get our homework done early."

"You have lots of rules," said Emma. "We only have three rules. That's enough."

"Only three?" asked Aunt Evelyn. "What are they?"

Emma leaned her chin in her hand. "Number one: Be kind. Number two: No kicking or biting. Number three: Any rule can be changed."

Aunt Evelyn smiled. "You're right. Maybe that is just about enough rules."

Aunt Evelyn took some knitting out of a large bag. The knitting was bright purple with shiny silver spangles on it. Emma thought it was very jazzy.

"What are you knitting?" she asked.

"Baby booties," said Aunt Evelyn. "For the baby."

"What baby?"

"Our baby, your Uncle Elliot's and mine," said Aunt Evelyn. "It's kind of a secret."

"Does Uncle Elliot know?" asked Emma.

"Yes," said Aunt Evelyn. "Uncle Elliot knows. And you, and your mother and father. That's about all."

Emma thought about the new baby. She pictured it looking like Aunt Evelyn, short curly black hair, three earrings, purple spangled booties. It would be, Emma knew, a very jazzy baby. And it would have lots and lots of rules. Emma watched as Aunt Evelyn took one finished spangled bootie out of her knitting bag. The bootie was extremely large, almost large enough for Emma. Emma looked at the silver spangles. She thought a moment.

"Aunt Evelyn, I'm very glad about your baby."

"Ditto," said Aunt Evelyn.

"What does ditto mean?" asked Emma.

"It means 'me too,'" said Aunt Evelyn.

"Aunt Evelyn," said Emma, "I have something bad to tell you."

"What's that?" asked Aunt Evelyn.

"Your baby will eat those spangles." Emma pointed to the baby booties.

"Oh dear," said Aunt Evelyn. "I suppose you are right. I don't know very much about babies."

Emma felt sorry for Aunt Evelyn.

"Don't worry, Aunt Evelyn, I was a baby about seven years ago. And my mother told me what I was like."

Aunt Evelyn put her arm around Emma. "You'd better tell me all about it," she said.

"First of all," Emma began, "babies don't pay attention to rules. They will eat spangles on booties, and wet and spit up milk and cry and wake up and sleep whenever they want to."

Aunt Evelyn sighed. "That's true, isn't it?"

Emma nodded. She looked at the purple spangled booties.

"Aunt Evelyn, I have something more bad to tell you."

"Now what?" asked Aunt Evelyn.

"Those purple booties are much too big for your baby," said Emma. "But I have some in my room that I saved from when I was a baby. They are not purple. I could give them to you."

Aunt Evelyn smiled at Emma. "Only if you want to, Emma."

Emma went into her room and found the booties. They were pink and blue. And they were very small. Aunt Evelyn loved them.

"Emma," she said, "I have noticed something. I think the purple spangled booties will fit you."

"I knew that," said Emma.

Aunt Evelyn laughed. "Oh, Emma. I like you."

"Ditto," said Emma.

After a while Uncle Elliot and Zachary came back from running. Zachary was carrying Wayne's leash. Uncle Elliot was carrying Wayne. He put Wayne down and Wayne found his favorite sun spot on the floor and lay down. Uncle Elliot lay down on the couch.

"That was fun," said Zachary.

"No, it was not fun," said Uncle Elliot. "That dog wouldn't run."

"I know," said Emma. "Wayne has his own rules and they are not about exercising. They are about sitting, lying down, sleeping, and eating."

"Just like babies," said Aunt Evelyn.

"Could I exercise with you tonight, Uncle Elliot?" asked Zach.

Uncle Elliot moaned. "I don't know, Zach. I'm so tired that I may have to break my rule about exercising twice a day."

"That's all right, dear," said Aunt Evelyn. "Rules can be changed."

"Now *that's* a wonderful rule," said Uncle Elliot with lots of feeling.

"I think so, too," said Aunt Evelyn.

"Ditto," said Emma.

From
Jasper and the Hero Business
by Betty Horvath

7

Jasper really wants to be a hero. But how can he be a hero in a neighborhood with no emergencies?!

Jasper lived in the house on the corner. It was a busy corner. All day long people passed by, hurrying to work, hurrying home again.

Jasper didn't hurry. He didn't have any place to go. Sometimes he didn't have anything to do. He watched the people pass by.

Sometimes they stopped and talked to him. They asked him questions.

There was one question that EVERYBODY asked him. "What are you going to be when you grow up?"

"I'm going to be a hero," Jasper said.

And then they laughed.

"Wait and see," thought Jasper. "Someday I am going to be a big hero. I will have my picture in the paper."

"OK, Jasper the Hero," said his brother Paul, "I have a job for you."

"This is no job for a hero," said Jasper. But he carried out the garbage anyway.

Then he went back to sit under his tree and wait for something brave to do.

A fire engine went clanging by.

"There goes a hero," said Jasper. "Off to do brave deeds and help people in trouble."

That night the newspaper had a picture of a fireman. He was carrying a baby down a ladder. Jasper cut the picture out of the paper.

That's the way his hero board began.

Every time Jasper read about someone being brave he pinned the story to the board on his bedroom wall.

"Someday," said Jasper, "my picture will be up there, too."

He was saving a place for it.

"There is never anything dangerous going on around here," said Jasper.

"That's good," said his mother. "Let's keep it that way."

Jasper took Rover for a walk.

Then he saw somebody running down the street.

"Maybe there has been a robbery," Jasper thought. "Maybe this is a thief coming! When he gets closer Rover and I can catch him. Maybe Rover will even bite him!"

But then the runner got closer. Jasper saw

it was Mr. Brown out doing his jogging. He patted Rover's head.

Rover wagged his tail.

"Some adventure!" thought Jasper.

He turned the corner. Right there on the ground was a piece of paper. It was money!

"If I can't be brave," said Jasper, "it's good to be rich."

When he got to the next corner, he heard
somebody crying. It sounded like someone
was in trouble. Maybe even in danger!

"Here's my chance to be a hero," said
Jasper.

But then he saw the little boy. He was
standing in front of Jasper's house. Not even
bleeding or anything.

"Are you lost?" Jasper asked. "Can I take
you home?"

Jasper could see it now. Headlines in the paper. HERO RETURNS LOST CHILD.

"No," sobbed the little boy, "*I'm* not lost. My money's lost."

Jasper sighed. "I found some money," he said. "I guess it's yours."

The little boy took it. He didn't say anything. He just watched Jasper and Rover go into the house.

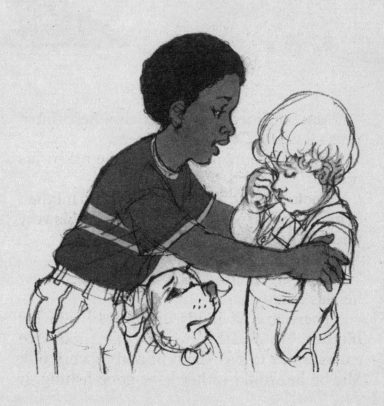

"Maybe I'm going about this hero business all wrong," thought Jasper.

"Do you know any heroes?" he asked his mother.

"Look out the window," said his mother. "There is a hero coming up the walk this very minute."

Jasper ran to the window.

"That's just Father," he said. "I never knew he was a hero."

"There are all kinds of heroes," said his mother. "Your father worked hard today to earn money to pay the rent and grocery bill. Maybe he would rather have gone fishing. It is a lucky family who has a hero like your father."

"Then I will put his picture on my hero board," said Jasper.

So Jasper found a picture of his father. Then he pinned his mother's picture up beside it.

But there was still the empty place where his picture belonged. He was getting older every minute. Another day was almost gone. Jasper wasn't a hero yet.

While they were eating dinner, the doorbell rang.

Jasper's father came back carrying a bunch of flowers.

"These are for you," he said.

"Jasper has a girl!" said Paul.

"No," said his father, "it was a little boy. He said Jasper gave him some money."

"Oh *him!*" said Jasper. "I *found* some money, but it was his. I just gave it back to him."

Nobody said anything for a minute. Then Paul said, "I bet that little boy thinks Jasper is a hero."

"Who, me? A hero?"

"Sure," said Paul. "If somebody *thinks* you're a hero, you *are* one. It is time to pin your picture on the hero board."

Paul helped him pin the picture up. Under it they wrote, "Jasper the Hero." The board was finished now. There was no more empty space.

From
New Neighbors for Nora
by Johanna Hurwitz

7

If only there were more children in Nora's apartment building. Besides seven-year-old Nora and her little brother Teddy, four-year-old Russell and his new baby sister are the only other kids. Will Nora's wish ever come true? Will a special best friend her own age ever move in?

From time to time an immense van would pull up in front of the building where Nora lived. The presence of the van meant that someone was either moving in or out of the house. Nora loved to watch the strong men carrying the furniture. Imagine a truck big enough to hold all the furniture from four or five rooms. The truck was big enough to live in! It was sad when someone moved away because then Nora was losing friends. But the arrival of new people was always exciting.

Now, however, the newest person to arrive was Russell's baby sister, Elisa. Nora liked her very much, but she had not done much growing yet. Nora couldn't remember when she or Teddy had been babies. She hadn't remembered that growing took so long. Whenever Nora saw her, Elisa was either sleeping or crying. Obviously it would be a long, long time before they could play together, and that was a big disappointment.

So Nora kept hoping that an already grown girl, just her size, would move into an empty apartment. Her wish would have to happen sometime. She just knew it.

One sunny Saturday in March, a new family did move into the building. Nora and Teddy, standing on the curb and peering into the truck, tried to count how many beds there were. But it was dark inside, and all the pieces of furniture were piled on top of each other. They fitted together like the three-dimensional puzzle that Teddy had gotten for his last birthday.

Nora and Teddy kept watching for a clue. Did the new tenants have children? All families have tables and chairs and chests of drawers. There was a sofa, two armchairs, and a desk. Just when it looked as if there were no clues for them at all, one of the movers emerged from the truck carrying a big carton. On one side of it someone had written the word *Toys*. Nora spelled it out for Teddy because he couldn't read yet.

"Grown-ups don't play with toys!" she said with delight. There had to be a child. And then, from the rear of the truck, one of the movers carried out a tiny, doll-sized rocking chair. That was what Nora had been waiting for. It was the absolute proof that the new family had a child and the child was a girl.

Nora wondered what she looked like and what she was named. She was certain that this girl was the special best friend she had been waiting for.

Nora and Teddy looked around them. The movers were closing up the now-empty truck, but there was no sign of the new tenants. Perhaps they were already upstairs in their new home. The new people would be living in apartment 4E. Nora and Teddy lived in 7E, exactly three floors above.

Nora couldn't wait to introduce herself to the new neighbors. But Mommy felt they should be given a little more time to move their furniture about and unpack their boxes. So not until eleven-thirty the next morning did Nora go with her mother and Teddy to greet the new people. They rang the doorbell and waited.

The door was opened by a tall man with

glasses. Mommy explained that they were neighbors and welcomed him to the building. As they stood in the doorway, the man was joined by a woman. He said, "This is my wife, Mrs. Eastman. I'm Mr. Eastman."

"Won't you come in?" invited Mrs. Eastman.

Nora looked about for the girl she knew would be there. It was strange to walk into an apartment that looked exactly like her own and yet was different at the same time. The Eastmans' sofa was facing in the opposite direction from the one in Nora's living room, but the kitchen was in the same place and looked identical except for the curtains.

"How old are you?" Mrs. Eastman asked Nora. "You are probably the same age as Gene."

Nora heard the name and smiled. She was right. There was a girl: Jean. There was a girl named Jean in her class at school, too.

"I'm seven years old," said Nora proudly. She was about to ask where Jean was when she heard the toilet in the bathroom down the hall being flushed. Then two things happened almost at once. Nora noticed the little tiny rocking chair in a corner of the living room with an old-fashioned-looking doll sitting in it. And at the same moment a *boy* came walking into the room. He was tall and wore glasses and looked very much like Mr. Eastman. Nora wondered if he was Jean's brother.

"This is our son Eugene Spencer," said Mrs. Eastman. "Gene was just eight years old."

This was Jean! Nora was stunned into silence. Gene was a boy. She could not believe it, and yet there he was standing right in front of her.

Mrs. Eastman said that she was having a problem with the stove, and the three adults walked off toward the kitchen. Nora stood looking at this new boy. She remembered that his mother said that he was eight years old. She herself had been seven for only a short while and was going to remain seven for quite a long time. When she was playing with Teddy and Russell, seven seemed very old and important. But suddenly seven didn't seem very old. This was not the way Nora had imagined things at all.

"Why do you have two names?" she asked Eugene Spencer.

"One for each of my grandfathers," Eugene said proudly. "One is named Spencer and the other is named Eugene, and we didn't want to hurt their feelings."

Nora had only one grandfather. Not counting her last name, she had only one name, too.

"I have two names," said Teddy, beaming. "Teddy and Theodore."

"They're both the same," said Nora. "Teddy is just a short way of saying Theodore. It's not your real name. It's a nick-name."

"My nickname is Gene," said Eugene Spencer, "but most people call me Eugene Spencer."

Eugene Spencer had everything: two grandfathers, two real names, *and* a nickname. Nora began to feel angry.

"If you're a boy," she asked, "why do you have a doll and a doll's chair?"

"That doll is an antique. It's very valuable and nobody plays with it," said Eugene Spencer. "It's just for looking at, so don't you touch it. It belonged to my great-grandmother when she was a little girl."

"Do you have a great-grandmother, too?" asked Nora. This awful boy seemed to have everything. She didn't have to look further in the apartment to know that he had his own bedroom down the hall.

"No, she died before I was born. She'd be

over one hundred years old if she was still alive. And this doll is one hundred years old. That's why it's an antique," he explained importantly.

"Do you have a fairy godmother?" asked Teddy.

"Don't be silly," said Eugene Spencer. "Nobody has a fairy godmother, except in silly stories."

"Stories aren't silly," retorted Nora. "And Teddy and I have a pretend fairy godmother. Her name is Mrs. Ellsworth, and she lives right here in this building. Sometimes she stays with us when our parents go out in the evening, and then we play make-believe magic."

"Aren't there any boys in this building?" asked Eugene Spencer. "In my old building we had twin brothers, just my age."

"I am a boy," said Teddy. "And Russell is a boy, too. He has a new baby sister, but she's too little to play yet."

"How old is Russell?" asked Eugene Spencer, looking interested.

"Four," said Nora.

"He's a baby. I don't play with babies."

"He's not a baby. He's our friend," said Nora. "We have lots of friends in this build-

ing. There's Mrs. Wurmbrand. We call her Mrs. W. She's like an extra grandmother to us." Nora thought for a minute. "How many grandmothers do you have?"

"Two," said Eugene Spencer.

"Well, counting Mrs. Wurmbrand, Teddy and I have three grandmothers. I don't think Mrs. Wurmbrand would be a grandmother for you. She would probably think that *you* are a baby. She is almost eighty-six years old."

"I'm older than you," said Eugene Spencer. "Besides, I don't need any more grandmothers."

He was quiet for a minute, and then he said, "Don't you want to see my room?"

Nora wanted to say no, but she was curious in spite of herself. So she and Teddy followed him down the hallway. His room was the one that Mommy and Daddy shared upstairs. There was a pair of bunk beds along one wall. Eugene Spencer seemed to have two of everything.

"Who sleeps in the other part of your bed?" Nora asked.

"No one," Eugene Spencer said. "Sometimes I sleep on top and sometimes I sleep on the bottom, whichever I feel like."

For some time Nora had been wishing for

a room all to herself. But now she said, "It sounds lonely to me. Teddy and I can talk to each other in the nighttime."

Mommy called to the children. It was time for them to go back to their own apartment. "We just wanted to welcome you," she said to the Eastmans. "I'm sure you will like living here very much."

Nora didn't care if they liked it here or not. In fact, if they didn't like it perhaps they would move again, and the girl she had been waiting for would come. She didn't like Eugene Spencer one bit. He was a show-off, just because he was older than she was and had two names.

When they returned to their apartment, Nora said to her mother, "I wish I had two names."

"Nora is such a lovely name that Daddy and I didn't think you needed another," her mother answered.

"Then call me Nora-Nora," said Nora.

"Sometimes I do," said Mommy.

Sure enough, in the evening when it was time for Nora's bath her mother had to call, "Nora-Nora! The water is ready now." And again when it grew late she had to say, "Nora-Nora! It's time for bed."

But in the afternoon when she asked, "Do

you want some milk and cookies, Nora?" she only had to say the name once.

Before they fell asleep in their beds that night, Teddy said, "Nora, guess what! Now that Eugene Spencer lives here, you're not the oldest child in the building anymore."

"So what!" said Nora. "It doesn't matter at all."

But it did. To Nora it mattered a whole lot.

From
Song Lee in Room 2B
by Suzy Kline

7

Song Lee is the shyest person in Doug's second-grade class. Everyone in Room 2B knows that. But there might be some things about Song Lee that would surprise them, too.

Miss Mackle looked out the window of Room 2B. "It's snowing in March?"

Harry jumped out of his seat. "Hot dog! Come and see, Doug."

"All right!" I said, slapping Harry five. It was fun watching the snow stick to the playground and treetops.

When I turned around, everybody was up at the windows.

Except Song Lee.

The teacher smiled at her. "You have permission to leave your seat."

"Thank you, Miss Mackle."

Miss Mackle sighed. "I wish everyone in our second-grade class had your good manners, Song Lee."

"STOP PUSHING!" Dexter shouted.

Harry held up a fist. "Make me, lizard breath."

"Harry and Dexter are fighting," Sidney called.

Miss Mackle waved her hands in the air. "That's it! Everyone sit down."

Harry and I shot Sidney a look. His tattling always got us in trouble.

After we returned to our seats, Miss Mackle looked at the class.

No one was smiling.

Most of us were moaning.

"I think we all have a case of cabin fever," Miss Mackle said.

"What's that?" Mary asked.

"It happens when people are cooped up in one place for a long time. Everyone gets grumpy."

"*GGGGGrrrrr,*" Harry growled, as he stood up and dangled his arms like a monster.

Song Lee giggled.

"I wish I could fly this coop and go to Texas," I grumbled.

Miss Mackle snapped her fingers. "Doug, you just gave me an idea! It's time for Room 2B to take a vacation."

"YEAH!" we all shouted.

Mary counted the days on our bird calendar. "How can we? Spring break is two weeks away."

Miss Mackle held up the globe, and spun it once. "The mind can take you anywhere! For homework tonight, each one of you will prepare a talk, and take us to your favorite vacation spot. Tell us what it is like. Bring in family pictures, maps, or brochures if you have them."

"I never go anywhere," I groaned.

"Me, either," Sidney replied.

Song Lee raised her hand. She looked like she was going to cry.

"Yes?" Miss Mackle said.

"I feel sick."

I looked at Song Lee. She wasn't really

73

sick. She just didn't want to stand in front of the class and give a talk.

Whenever the class had a play, Song Lee had a silent part, like a dead fish or Little Miss Muffet.

Miss Mackle put her hand on Song Lee's forehead. "You aren't warm. Is your stomach bothering you?"

Song Lee nodded. "I feel sick and sad all morning."

"Really? A moment ago you were giggling at Harry."

Song Lee looked down at her desk.

Miss Mackle patted her head. "Don't worry, Song Lee. You can give a short little talk tomorrow."

When the teacher left, Song Lee took out her pink cherry-blossom handkerchief.

"Are you crying?" I asked.

Song Lee sniffed a few times.

When she caught her breath she whispered, "If I don't give talk tomorrow, I get zero on homework chart."

"Don't worry," Harry said, putting his elbow on my desk. "You'll never have as many zeros as me."

I looked over at the homework chart. Song Lee's row of red stars was twice as long as Harry's. "Gee, you've *never* gotten a zero!"

Song Lee wiped her eyes. "I don't feel well. I stay home . . . write story about vacation. Mother bring story in and Miss Mackle give me red star on yellow homework chart."

"If you stay home, you'll miss my talk," I said.

"And *mine,*" Harry added, flashing his white teeth and making his thick eyebrows go up and down.

Song Lee giggled.

Harry could always make her laugh. Even now, when she had tears in her eyes.

"You *have* to come tomorrow," we said.

The next morning when the bell rang, Song Lee was not in her seat. The words PUBLIC SPEAKING were written on the board. By 9:30, five people had already talked about Disney World, Sea World, and Epcot Center. Lots of brochures were passed around. Posters and souvenirs were displayed on the chalkboard.

Sidney showed us some neat pictures of a barbecue on his back porch. He and his stepdad were wearing chef hats and cooking hamburgers.

When it was my turn, I put on Grampa's ten-gallon hat, got out Grandma's book about Texas, and started talking.

"I've never been to Texas but I'm going

someday. Someday, I'm going to be the rootinest, the tootinest, and the shootinest cowboy ever to raise the dust on a high Texas plain."

When I was showing a picture of a rodeo, Song Lee and her mother appeared at the door, so I stopped talking.

"Hello, Mrs. Park," the teacher said.

Song Lee was not smiling when she dashed to her seat.

After Miss Mackle talked with Mrs. Park in the hall, the teacher returned. "Go on, Doug," she said.

So I did.

"You can visit the LBJ Ranch in Texas. LBJ are initials for Lyndon B. Johnson. He was president after Kennedy was shot. This is a picture of the Alamo."

Miss Mackle smiled when I sat down. "I liked the way Doug had bookmarks in his book to show us special places in Texas. He was very organized. And his hat was fun. Who would like to go next?"

We all looked at Song Lee. She shook her head. "I . . . go . . . last."

"Harry?" Miss Mackle called.

Harry walked up to the front of the room with a souvenir book. I had seen it hundreds of times. It was about the House on the Rock in Wisconsin.

"You walk out on this long narrow beam and see the hills and trees below. Mom said it was creepy because the beam teetered. I thought it was fun."

Miss Mackle shivered. "You're . . . very brave, Harry."

Harry grinned.

Twenty minutes later, it was time for the last person to speak. Miss Mackle tried to be casual about it. "Eh . . . let's see, Song Lee, I guess you're next."

Slowly, Song Lee got out of her seat. She

walked up to the little wooden stand that sat on a desk and had a sign that said PODIUM.

Mary and Ida smiled at their friend.

Harry and I shook our heads. There was no way she was going to do this.

Song Lee took one look at the class and then ran out to the hallway.

I knew it!

Everyone looked at the teacher.

I thought she'd get mad. But she didn't. She just sat at the side of the room.

Waiting.

Then something appeared in the doorway.

It was a big piece of cardboard that had a brown trunk, branches, lots of leaves, and a dozen pink Kleenex flowers.

Harry and I pointed at the round holes that were cut out for eyes, nose, mouth, and hands.

"SONG LEE!" we all shouted as the tree moved across the classroom to the podium.

I stared at the two pink lips in the mouth-hole of the tree. They were beginning to move.

"I was born in Seoul, Korea . . . where Summer Olympics take place in 1988."

"Would the tree speak louder, please?" Miss Mackle said with a big smile.

When Song Lee nodded, the pink Kleenex flowers jiggled.

"Korea is size of Virginia. It is like Switzerland because it has many mountain and beautiful blue sky. There are many palace, royal tomb, secret garden, and stone pagoda. We also have 3,000 island in Korea."

"Ooooh," the class replied.

Song Lee continued, "It is ten o'clock in

Room 2B. In Korea, grandmother Bong sleep. It is midnight in Seoul."

Mary made some tally marks on a piece of paper. "Korea is 14 hours ahead of us!"

Song Lee shook the branches and made her green leaves and pink blossoms quiver. "In spring, we have many picnic under

cherry tree at Korean park. My family play Ping-Pong and archery."

Harry stood up and shot a pretend arrow at Sidney. *"BOING!"*

Song Lee giggled. "It is time now for cherry-blossom tree to leave."

Everyone cheered as Song Lee scooted outside to the hallway.

Miss Mackle went over to the yellow homework chart and added another star for Song Lee. This time it was a gold one!

As soon as Song Lee returned to her seat, she covered her face.

"Your talk was great!" I said.

Harry clapped. "You're the best tree in the world."

When she spread her fingers apart, I could see she was smiling.

I found out one thing about Song Lee that day. She may be shy, but she can sure surprise you.

From
Don't Call Me Beanhead!
by Susan Wojciechowski

7

Meet Beany (or Bernice Sherwin-Hendricks on paper — or when her mother is mad). Beany worries that when she rides a Ferris wheel her car will come unhooked. She worries that if she leaves her seat at the movies to go get popcorn, she'll never find it again. Once she had a rash on her thumb and worried that it would fall off. Now she's losing another tooth. Will this be a whole new thing to worry about?

One of my teeth came out right in the middle of lunch at school. It was a bottom tooth — two teeth to the left of the middle one — and it came out when I bit into an apple. I wrapped the tooth in a napkin and put it in my lunch box. During math I went to the nurse, Mrs. Facinelli, to show her my tooth and look at her wall chart of an eyeball.

On the bus ride home I showed the tooth to Carol Ann.

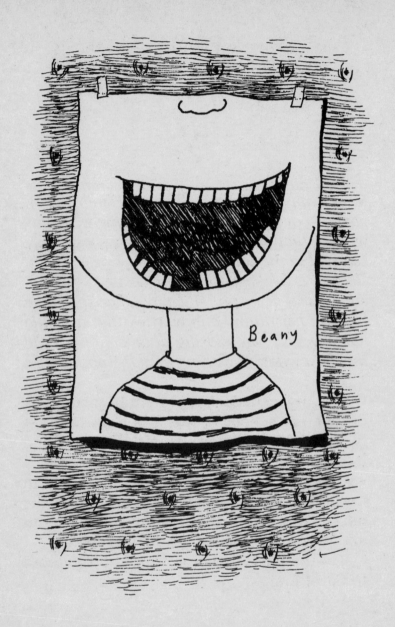

Beany

"How much do you get for a tooth?" she asked.

"Fifty cents," I said. "How much do you get?"

"I get seventy-five," she said, and grinned kind of a bragging grin. I hate it when she does that.

"No fair! How come you get so much more than me?"

"Do you floss?" Carol Ann asked.

"Sometimes. Well, only the day before I go to get my teeth cleaned."

"Do you leave a thank-you note under your pillow?"

"I didn't know you're supposed to. How come nobody ever tells me this stuff?"

"Okay, I'm going to help you out," Carol Ann said. "I'm going to tell you a list of rules I made up. Number one, soak your tooth in Polident false teeth cleaner for one hour till the dried-up blood comes out of the hole in the middle of the tooth."

"I don't have any Polident," I said.

"I'll give you some of my grandfather's." Carol Ann's grandfather lives with them. He has false teeth, but he doesn't wear them, except for church. Most of the time he keeps them in a peanut butter jar on the kitchen sink. I couldn't eat peanut butter for a week after I first saw Mr. Devlin's teeth soaking in that jar.

"Okay, what comes after the Polident?" I asked.

"Number two, brush the tooth with toothpaste. Number three, cover the tooth with clear nail polish to make it shine. Number four, leave the tooth under your pillow in a special box just for teeth."

"I don't have one!" I said when I heard number four. I started to bite my nails.

"Well, make one. Don't you know any-thing?" Carol Ann sighed and went on listing the rules. "Number five — and this is very important — leave a thank-you note under your pillow."

I asked Carol Ann if she would write down what she says in her thank-you notes.

She sighed again and said, "Oh, all right." I watched over her shoulder as she pulled a sheet of filler paper out of her backpack and wrote:

Dear Tooth Fairy,

Thank you for paying me for my tooth. I will not buy candy with the money. I floss every day.

From,
Carol Ann

PS: My sister Margo does not floss every day even if she says she does.

I stopped at Carol Ann's house on the way home from the bus stop. She gave me a plastic sandwich bag of Polident.

At supper I passed my tooth around the table so everyone could see it.

"It looks just like a little pearl," my mother said.

"It looks strong and healthy because you drink lots of milk," my father said.

"Gross. Get that thing out of my face," my brother said.

"I really think this tooth is worth seventy-five cents," I told everyone at the table.

That night, after I showed the tooth to Jingle Bell, I made a tooth box out of construction paper. Then I put all the things I would need on the bathroom sink. I put the box, a glass of water mixed with Polident, a toothpick and a safety pin for digging out the blood from the little hole in the middle of the tooth, a toothbrush and a tube of tartar control toothpaste so the tooth wouldn't get any plaque, and a bottle of Flaming Fuchsia nail polish. Carol Ann had said to use clear polish, but all I had was Flaming Fuchsia that my grandmother bought me when I stayed at her house one weekend. My mother told me Flaming Fuchsia is a teenage color, so I haven't used it yet.

I turned on the water and held my tooth under it to get off the bits of napkin and my brother's fingerprints, and then it happened: My tooth went down the drain.

For a few seconds I couldn't believe what had happened. Then I started yelling, "Emergency, emergency!" over and over again, until my parents and Philip came running up the stairs, asking if I was hurt or if I was sick. Philip wanted to call 911.

My dad turned off the water and took apart all the pipes under the sink. But the tooth wasn't there. Philip said it was probably already miles away in the sewer, being eaten by a rat. My mother said, "Philip

Jerome Sherwin-Hendricks, go to your room."

Then she sat on the toilet lid holding me in her lap and telling me everything would be all right.

That night my pillow was very lumpy. Underneath it I had put an empty tooth box, a note I wrote to the tooth fairy explaining about the tooth going down the drain, my thank-you note, a picture I drew of my mouth showing what spot the tooth came from, a picture of our bathroom sink after the pipes had been taken apart, and a poem I wrote.

Here are the pictures:

Here is the poem:

HOW I LOST MY TOOTH

I wiggled it and jiggled it

and squiggled it.

I couldn't get it out.

I pushed it and pulled it and turned it

I couldn't get it out

I couldn't get it out but my apple did.

I bit it and cried.

My tooth was inside,

All covered with blood.

Then it went down the sink

And that stinks.

The next morning at the bus stop Carol Ann asked me how much I got.

"My usual fifty cents," I said.

"Well, hand it over. My grandfather blew his top when he looked for his Polident and it was all gone. We have to buy him a new box."

From
Sophie Is Seven
by Dick King-Smith

7

From the time she was four, Sophie wanted to be one thing: a farmer. By the time she was six, she not only had a flock of snails and a herd of centipedes, but a cat named Tomboy, a rabbit named Beano, and a puppy named Puddle. Now, at last, it is Christmas — and her birthday — and Sophie is seven. That means Sophie can finally take something every farmer should — her first riding lessons — thanks to her great-great-aunt Al.

Christmas Day came and went. For Sophie it had the usual bonus — two presents from each person, one with "Merry Christmas" on it, one with "Happy Birthday."

But Sophie had made sure that the other members of the family were not forgotten. She had raided her Farm Money and had bought what she thought were suitable gifts.

For her father — a large box of matches,

to help him light that pipe of his that seemed always to be going out.

For her mother — a large bar of Lifebuoy soap. ("Not that you aren't quite clean, Mom," she said, "but this smells different from our usual stuff.")

For Matthew and Mark — sweets, as usual.

For Tomboy — a piece of coley from the fishmonger. ("Its real name is coalfish," he had told her. "Good," said Sophie. "Just right for a coal-black cat.")

For Puddle — a big bone from the butcher.

For Beano — the biggest carrot at the grocer's.

For only one person had Sophie not bought anything, and that was the person who was going to give her the biggest, most expensive present ever, the course of riding lessons.

How could she compete with that? Whatever should she get Aunt Al? After Christmas she consulted her mother, who thought for a while and then said, "You know, rather than buying her something, I think that what Aunt Al would like best would be if you made her something, did it all by yourself, just for her, a special present."

"I can't make things," Sophie said. "I'm no good at that."

"I know!" her mother said. "Write her a poem. You did a lovely poem for your farming topic — your teacher showed me. Do one for Aunt Al."

"What about?"

"Well, it could be part of a Christmas card. You could draw a picture and write a poem, too."

"But Christmas is over."

"Well, a New Year card then."

"Okay," Sophie said. "I'll have a go."

She did the picture first. After a lot of thought, she decided to draw a black cat. Cats weren't as hard to do as some things, and it was easy to color it in with a black felt marker. Of course she drew it walking from right to left. Then she wrote OLLIE under it. The poem took longer, but Sophie worked away determinedly at it, occasionally asking questions like, "What rhymes with 'Scotland'?" or, "What rhymes with 'the Highlands'?" or, "How old's Aunt Al going to be next year?"

At last she finished it, the day before Aunt Al was due to arrive. To Sophie's surprise, her father set off quite early on the morning of December the thirty-first to fetch his great-aunt from the railway station.

"The train's due in at nine A.M.," he said.

96

"Yikes!" cried Sophie. "You said she lived six hundred miles away. If she only started out this morning, it must be the fastest train in the world."

"No, no," her father said. "It's a ten-hour journey, but she has a sleeping compartment, you see. She'll have slept nearly all the way, I hope."

And indeed when Aunt Al did arrive, she looked as fresh as a daisy. Sophie waited till everyone else had gone off to do something or other, and then she produced her special present.

"I did this for you," she said. "It took an awful long time."

Aunt Al took the card in her skinny, bony old hands, curled like a bird's claws, and looked at the picture of the black cat, and read beneath it:

This is a poem for you Aunt Al
Because you are my speshial pal
And this year Mommy told me
You are going to be 83
So I wish you a Happy New Year

And I hope you will have a nice stay here
Where it is warmer than Scotland
Which is not a hot land
Speshially on top of the Highlands
The coldest place in the British Ilands
And the picture is of Ollie
And you can see his sister Dolly
Because she lives at Cloverlea
Riding Stables where I shall be
Going to ride on Saturday
And you are going to pay
So I am very pleased
With love from your great great neece

"It's a very good poem, Sophie," Aunt Al
said.

"It is, isn't it," Sophie said.

"And it rhymes beautifully."

"It does, doesn't it."

"And it's the very nicest present you could
have given me," said Aunt Al. "I shall treasure
it. And talking of treasuring things, I brought
something to show you."

She rummaged in her handbag and brought out an old snapshot.

"Have a look at that," she said.

Sophie took the photograph and studied it. It was not very clear and the picture was rather brownish, but she could see that it was of a small girl sitting on a pony.

"Who d'you think that is?" Aunt Al asked.

"Don't know," said Sophie. "Nobody I know."

"Turn it over then," said Aunt Al, so Sophie did, and written on the back in rather spidery and faded grown-up's writing was:

Alice on Frisk
Balnacraig 1920

"It's you!" Sophie said.

"Yes. I was nine."

"And was Frisk your pony?"

"Yes. He was rather a naughty pony but I loved him more than anything in the world."

"More than your mom and dad?"

"Well, no, perhaps not. But next best after them."

"I wish I could have a pony of my own," said Sophie.

"Wait till you're a lady farmer," said Aunt Al, "and then have a horse, that's my advice. Now tell me — your first lesson is tomorrow, is that right?"

"Yes. It's not really the first. I did some riding in Cornwall."

"How much do you know about the tack?"

"Well," said Sophie, "there's a bridle and reins and a saddle. Oh, and a thing around the pony's tummy."

"The girth. What about a snaffle, what's that?"

"Don't know."

"It's a kind of bit, that goes in the horse's mouth, but it's jointed, so it isn't as harsh as a curb. And what's a numnah?"

"Don't know."

"It's a cloth or pad, a sheepskin sometimes, that goes under the saddle to stop it chafing."

"Gosh, you know a lot, Aunt Al," Sophie said.

"I was a good horsewoman once. Shall I tell you what I think will happen tomorrow?"

"Yes, please."

"Well, you'll all be riding your ponies inside an enclosed ring called a menage, and all around this ring there will be posts at intervals, each with a big letter on it. A K E H C M B F."

"Why?"

"So that the instructor can say to you, 'Right, now ride across from A to M,' or 'E to B,' or whatever."

"Oh," said Sophie. "Do they always have those letters?"

"Yes," said Aunt Al, "and they always teach you the same way to remember them. 'All King Edward's Horses Can Manage Big Feeds.'"

"Oh," said Sophie. "I thought King Edward was a potato."

"Oh, Sophie," said Aunt Al. "You're definitely going to be a farmer."

From
Second-Grade Friends
by Miriam Cohen

7

It's a big day in Jacob's second-grade class, and Jacob is worried. A Real Author is coming to visit and read stories the students have written. What a time for Jacob to get his first case of writer's block!

A Real Author was coming to talk to second grade about how to be a writer and have imagination. Mrs. Rosebloom was going to put up their work in the hall so the Real Author could see what good writers they were.

Everybody was writing and writing, except Jacob. He put his head down on his desk, and started worrying. "In second grade you have to be much smarter than in first grade. You have to work, work, work, every minute. I can't do all this hard work! In first grade I was happy all the time."

Franky was busy with something under his desk. He grinned at Jacob. He was folding a piece of paper so it would make a fire-

cracker noise when he pulled it open. Franky never worried.

Gregory was writing a funny story. He stopped and poked Jacob. "Are you thinking again?" Gregory admired Jacob a lot. He was Jacob's real friend. "Why don't you start writing, Jacob? The Author is almost here," said Gregory.

Jacob touched Suzy on her back just a teeny bit with his pencil eraser. She turned around and stared at him through her new glasses. "Stop that!"

Jacob leaned over and whispered, "Hey, Nathan, you want to hear a good riddle?"

Nathan looked annoyed. "Jacob, I'm trying to work."

"I don't know why the kids don't like me as much as they used to," Jacob said to himself. "Probably they won't even come to my birthday party." Then he said to Franky, "I wish I was still in first grade."

"You're crazy!" said Franky.

The twins LaToya and LaTanya stopped writing. "The Real Author is coming, Jacob," said LaToya.

"We're going to get his autograph," said LaTanya.

"You'd better hurry, Jacob," they both

said. Then they put their heads down over their papers again.

Jacob liked the yellow plastic airplanes, blue teddy bears, and red hearts holding all their little pigtails. He was counting them when he saw Suzy looking at him through her glasses. They made her eyes look very big and smart.

She shook her head. "Jacob, you're not working. It's very important for a Real Author to meet you."

"Oh, yes," said Katy. "I just love a Real Author. Once my aunt was shopping, and she saw a Real Author, and she ran after him to get his autograph. But it was somebody else who wasn't even an author."

Jacob said, "I would like to write a book. But it would take too long. Besides, I might get the writer's cramp." Mrs. Rosebloom had told them how writers' hands could pinch up from too much writing.

"Yeah, or a headache," Gregory said. "Nathan's going to have a *big* headache. Look how much he wrote!" Nathan's story already went down two pages and halfway on another.

Jacob covered up his empty paper with his hand.

Mrs. Rosebloom told him. "Why don't you try a poem?" So Jacob decided to write one. Poems could be really short. He looked up at the ceiling. He drew pencil lines between the corduroy on his pants. Finally he thought of a poem:

> "I like my teacher.
> She is nice
> Because she isn't . . ."

It was really hard to think of what would rhyme with "nice." Then he thought of it — "pice."

"What is 'pice'?" LaToya and LaTanya asked.

"I don't know, but it rhymes," Jacob said.

Some of the kids laughed, because "pice" sounded so funny.

"The Real Author is coming to see your work in a few minutes," Mrs. Rosebloom told the class.

When Jacob heard Mrs. Rosebloom say that, he quickly chewed his poem into little pieces. Then he dropped them in the gerbils' cage. It was all right because gerbils have torn-up paper in the bottom of their cages anyway.

Honey was ready to read her story to the class. She was the biggest and roundest and strongest kid in second grade. She was also the nicest. Honey liked everyone. She always gave anybody who wanted one an extra-big cookie from her lunch.

"Class, let's all be ready to help Honey with her story," said Mrs. Rosebloom. "Remember, give your opinions in a kind way."

Honey began, "Once there was a cute little girl named Lou-Ann." (That was Honey's real name.) "She was the strongest in her whole class. But her stepmother said, 'There is a dance-ball, and you cannot go to it!' So she was crying in the kitchen. Then a fairy jumped out of the microwave and said, 'Come with me, and you will win a prize.'"

Suzy whispered very loud to Katy, "She's just copying Cinderella."

The teacher said, "Lots of fairy tales use those ideas, Suzy. And writers always put some of themselves in their stories." Then she sat down next to Honey. "Maybe you could try something that is not *quite* so much like Cinderella."

Mrs. Rosebloom turned around. "Have you written anything yet, Jacob?"

Jacob shook his head. He looked worried.

Katy told Jacob, "Once I didn't have any imagination, and I closed my eyes, and I got some."

Jacob closed his eyes.

"What do you see?" everybody wanted to know.

"I see . . . beavers," Jacob said. Once he and his dad watched a TV special about beavers, and Jacob got very interested in them. Every week he took out the same beaver book at library period.

"Beavers are boring," Franky laughed. "Jacob, you're *weird*!"

"Why don't you write about 'My Fishing Trip with My Father'?" said LaToya.

"I never went on a fishing trip with my father." Jacob would have loved to go fishing, but his father wasn't really that kind of a father.

"Well, what *do* you do with your father?" LaTanya asked.

"Sometimes we read together on the sofa. He reads his newspaper, and I read my library book."

"Well, what happens then?"

"We just read, and breathe," said Jacob.

"You should get your father to play some baseball with you," said LaTanya.

"Like ours does," said LaToya.

Jacob didn't want to mention it, but his father didn't know how to play baseball.

Honey was getting bored working on her story. She smiled at Jacob. In kindergarten, Honey used to put Jacob in the doll-buggy. "I'm the mommy, and you're the baby," she would say. It made Jacob very embarrassed.

Now, she came up behind him. "Hey, look at this! I can pick up Jacob *and* his chair!"

"Put me down!" Jacob shouted.

Mrs. Rosebloom hurried over. "Honey! You could hurt somebody doing that! Put him down this minute!"

Honey went back to her seat and waved at Jacob. Jacob was only mad for a little while. You couldn't stay mad at Honey because she liked you even when you were mad at her.

"My story is ready," Katy said. It was about her Pinky Pony. She really did have a Pinky Pony, just like the one on TV. In the story, Pinky Pony found the rainbow with her little friends, the rabbit, and Raggedy Ann, and "they all had a delicious party."

"I wrote a space science fiction novel," Nathan told the class.

"How many pages does it have?" asked Mrs. Rosebloom.

"Ten, so far," said Nathan.

"Wonderful!" Mrs. Rosebloom said. "But

we won't have time to read it out loud now. The Author will be here in just a few minutes. Finish your work quickly, class!"

"But I didn't write anything!" Jacob cried.

"Well, never mind, dear. You can hold the banner we made. It says, 'Welcome Author!' in such colorful letters."

Jacob scuffed his sneaker on the floor. He didn't answer. The teacher patted him, and hurried into the hall to put up their stories.

Jacob was almost crying. "I'm the only one with no imagination — I'll probably grow up without any imagination!"

"Don't make such a fuss," said Suzy. "You can still eat and walk around."

"Don't worry," Honey told him. "You want one of the cupcakes from my lunch?"

Jacob shook his head. "The Author won't even know I'm here! He'll think I can't do anything!"

"We'll tell him," Gregory said. "We'll tell him you can bend your thumb way back and touch your arm. You can show him."

"Why don't you just write about something you're interested in?" LaToya and La-Tanya said.

"It's too late! There's no time!" Jacob cried.

Katy ran and got Jacob's pencil and paper.

110

Gregory and Franky sat him down at his desk, and pushed the pencil into his hand. Suddenly Jacob began to write. His ideas kept coming. He almost couldn't write them down fast enough.

"That's the way, Jacob," everybody cheered. "Come on, Jacob!"

The minute Jacob finished, Mrs. Rosebloom put up his story in the hall.

"He's coming!" Everybody ran to peek out the door. The principal was smiling and smiling. She was walking next to the Author and telling him, "Our cafeteria was added in 1985."

"He's supposed to be bigger!" Franky said.

Suzy stared through her new glasses. "He doesn't look right."

Katy said, "He's not supposed to be so old."

Franky said, "Maybe it's not *really* him."

Little kindergarten children, in a line, waved and said, "Hi, Author!"

The Real Author began looking at second grade's stories. "This is so interesting," he said about Nathan's. "What a funny one!" he said about Gregory's. "I like the part about the fairy in the microwave," he said about Honey's story. Then he stopped in front of Jacob's paper. Jacob chewed on his jean jacket collar, he was so nervous.

"'Why Are There Beavers?'" read the Real Author. He smiled a lot and nodded while he was reading.

"He likes yours!" Gregory whispered to Jacob.

"All of these people have such good imaginations!" the Real Author said.

Gregory poked Jacob. "See, you've got imagination!"

Jacob said, "Well, maybe *sometimes* I do."

"Give yourself a pat on the back for fine work, Jacob," said Mrs. Rosebloom.

And Jacob did.